The Crooked Forest

Forest

CLOUD CRAZED

JONI FRANKS

To order additional copies of this book, contact:
Xlibris
844-714-8691
www.Xlibris.com
Orders@Xlibris.com

ISBN: Softcover   978-1-6698-7496-6
             Hardcover   978-1-6698-7498-0
             EBook   978-1-6698-7497-3

Library of Congress Control Number: 2023907671

Print information available on the last page

Rev. date: 04/25/2023

Books by Joni Franks

The Corky Tails: Tales of a Tailless Dog Named Sagebrush book series
Corky Tails
Sagebrush Meets the Shuns
Sagebrush and the Smoke Jumper
Sagebrush and the Butterfly Creek Flood
Sagebrush and the Warm Spring Discovery
Rabos Taponados
Corky Tails Coloring Book
Sagebrush and the Disappearing Dark Sky
Sagebrush and the Never Summer Mountains

The Crooked Forest book series
The Crooked Forest, Legacy of the Holey Stone
The Crooked Forest, Cloud-Crazed

For Sir Gyzmo
You have the heart of a hero

When we choose forgiveness
Our grief will melt away
Lessening our burdens
And brightening up our days

It is not a simple task
To heal a shattered heart
We must free the past forever
To create a fresh start

The Secret Passage

Luna woke with a start from deep within the tree hole she had sought refuge in the night before. Yesterday she had been chased by Aidan, the sheepherder, for what seemed like an eternity; and because of Aidan's fierce pursuit, she was now separated from her dear daughter, Willow.

The dim morning light entered through the small opening as Luna stirred within the nest of leaves that had kept her warm. She had spent the night in a fantastically large, crooked pine tree that was twisted at the roots with a curved arch near its base, deep within the heart of the Crooked Forest.

The rare and remote Crooked Forest was an ancient old growth forest, immeasurable in size, and home to the oldest life forms on earth. Despite the trees twisted shape, they remained resilient and hardy. Centuries ago, blizzards descended, freezing the young saplings into a bent over position as the heavy, wet snow weighed down the tree limbs so that they brushed the ground, forming an envelope of protection for the small creatures known as Shuns, like Luna, who called the Crooked Forest home.

It was a cloudy, rainy day with thick gray clouds that prevented any sunlight from entering the tree hole. The cold fat raindrops that plopped to the ground mimicked the feeling of loss Luna held in her heart. She would need to summon her inner strength to face this gloomy, lonely day.

Luna was in a weakened state, and she intuitively knew that she didn't possess the energy required to return to the place where she and Willow had become separated. She had been harvesting the mistletoe herb to treat the headaches that plagued her when Aidan began to hurl rocks at her. It seems she was breaking the law by gathering herbs, a rule put into place by the humans, and Aidan intended to enforce those laws. Luna felt a headache brewing now, and she wished for a hot cup of the medicinal tea that she could make from the precious mistletoe herb, had it not been for Aidan interrupting her efforts.

Sliding out of the tree hole to the ground, Luna's bare feet sensed the pulse of the earth's ley lines. Folklore spoke of the Crooked Forest being a portal to a parallel world due to natural energy bands that were located there. There was a magical, mystical alignment in this terrain, creating a place of great power, which seemed uncannily familiar to Luna.

As she approached a grouping of hefty boulders, Luna felt the earth tremor slightly. She was on what appeared to be a ceremonial pathway lined with a collection of exceptionally large vertical stones that were topped with horizontal balancing stones. She heard the whispered code that only those that were attuned to the ancient ways and nature's power can hear.

Taking one step forward, she suddenly felt herself tumble backwards, yet the ground was not there to meet her fall as she fell through space. The self that she once was disappeared, as she became suspended in time where she felt nothing and everything simultaneously.

"This is where time begins and ends," she heard a small, comforting voice say.

"There is no measure of time here, dear one," the voice continued. "Only the light is here that will heal and restore your worn and damaged body, Luna. Breathe in the light until it is time for you return to the person you are meant to be."

Aftermath

Aidan's life had changed immensely over the past years, and not for the better. Memories of what came before the drought had evaporated, just like Dragonfly Ditch, had evaporated right before his eyes on that distant fateful day.

Aidan rarely thought of Luna, or her daughter Willow and her pesky little dog, Sir Gyzmo who could practically fly. Since the drought his path had not crossed with any Shuns. Everything in the forest was different now than it had been before.

Consumed with survival for himself and his herd of sheep, life was harder than it ever needed to be. Nowadays, Aidan had to travel vast distances to locate water for himself and his flock.

Before the drought, Aidan had never shown any reverence or acceptance for the elemental beings that populated the Crooked Forest. Until that fateful day, he had remained oblivious to their existence. He had also believed that his native land was a never-ending resource for him to use as he saw fit, which had led to an environmental atrocity.

There had been a water crisis in his hometown of Flowerville due to the expanded population of humans, as they left life in the forest to pursue living closer together in huts and forming villages. Soon, Dragonfly Ditch could not provide enough water for them all.

So Aidan hatched a scheme to divert water from nearby Sleeping Creek into Dragonfly Ditch. He wanted the town folk of Flowerville to consider him a hero and a great and powerful magician, capable of diverting water by simply asking the water to move. The truth was he manipulated the earth with a digging tool, but his efforts failed.

His water diversion antics had been halted by the beautiful creature known as Dewdrop, the elemental water fairy of Sleeping Creek. As the protector of Sleeping Creek, Dewdrop prevented Aidan's misguided efforts by putting an end to his diversion scheme before it even began.

Frightened by this startling experience, as the truth of his actions were revealed to him, Aidan had been shown that ultimately, he was the one responsible for Dragonfly Ditch drying up and the once beautiful Flowerville being stricken with drought for the next seven generations to come.

There had been only one silver lining during the years that followed this event, but now even that once glorious experience had turned bitter. Aidan found himself missing his beautiful wife these days. She had recently vanished from their home after a fiery quarrel.

Remembering

Willow tossed and turned in a fitful sleep. In her dream, she clearly saw Aidan, armed with a pick and shovel, diligently digging a trench alongside Sleeping Creek. His brow was furrowed and sweat poured down his face as he hit the earth time and time again.

"Just a little deeper," Willow heard Aidan grunt. "I will have this water diverted in no time, and those peasants in Flowerville will think I'm a magician!"

Aidan had not considered that his diversion plan would alter the flow of Sleeping Creek, compromising the only water source the forest creatures had. Hitting the earth with his pick one final time, the waters of Sleeping Creek broke through, and the diversion trench channeled the precious water into Dragonfly Ditch.

Willow closed her eyes and steadied herself. "He must be stopped, and it must be now."

It was then that Willow's spirit animal, the silver wolf, appeared before Aidan. His sleek silver fur standing on end and a deep growl rumbled from his massive chest. The wolf's yellow eyes locked with Aidan's, and in that very instant, much became clear to the sheepherder.

"Abundance, prosperity, and health are granted by the elemental world when one upholds the greater good. Tragedy can ensue due to the imbalance of a life lived in darkness and lies" was the message the wolf conveyed before he suddenly shape-shifted into a stellar jay, squawking noisily, flying close to Aidan's face. Aidan had thrown down his pick, raising his arms to his face to protect himself from the bird's fluttering wings, as he clearly saw the warning of the disaster that was to come.

Willow abruptly awoke. The dream was over, but her heart was still racing.

As it turned out, this was the dawning of an entirely new era for the humans in Flowerville. Now, they felt the consequences of Dewdrop's power. In the blink of a fairy's eye, Dragonfly Ditch had dried up, leaving Flowerville stricken with drought, rendering it a dead zone.

Willow had been transformed from witnessing this profound event. Something had shifted inside of her, and she felt much older than her actual years. Thus far, her young life had resembled the gnarled and twisted branches of the Crooked Forest. Her journey filled with bumps and snags along the way.

She still remembered that tragic day when she had been separated from Luna. But, nowadays, Willow chose to remember the pleasant memories she had shared with her mother more than the heartbreaking recollection of their separation. She had learned that the event that had caused her such immense grief was the very challenge she had to overcome to realize her destiny as a heroine.

Legends

Willow and Sir Gyzmo were admired by the other forest creatures and the elementals for their courage, outstanding achievements, noble qualities, and great inner strength, which had become legend. Folktales of their adventures together grew, and others were inspired to live their lives in the same manner as they had.

Except for Aidan.

Willow and Sir Gyzmo's practices and reverence for nature irritated Aidan, and he would have been delighted if they were run out of the Crooked Forest forever. So Aidan pursued Willow and Sir Gyzmo relentlessly, just like he had pursued Luna.

But Willow and Sir Gyzmo had outwitted Aidan at every turn. Willow became an expert at effortlessly climbing onto Sir Gyzmo's fairy saddle that she had woven for him out of columbine and lavender flowers, and off the pair would go, nearly flying, as they escaped Aidan's fierce pursuit.

Sir Gyzmo wanted to give Willow something special to remind her of her mother. So he gifted her a mistletoe branch as a reminder for her to hold hope in her heart for Luna's return.

After Willow's separation from Luna, as if by magic, Sir Gyzmo had suddenly appeared. The fated arrival of her friend and trusted companion had helped Willow find the sunshine during the rain, as she struggled to move beyond the dark and dismal pain of her new reality without her mother.

Willow listened to the fairy dog's guidance and credited him for saving her from ultimate despair. To this day, she would remember his advice to her when she began to feel low.

"You must find hope for the future," Sir Gyzmo would wisely counsel her.

"Hope? How can I feel hopeful when I am so troubled?" Willow remembered herself crying.

"Hope is not pretending that troubles don't exist. It is finding optimism that the troubles won't last forever. Your aching heart will heal in time, and you will be ready to go forward, knowing that no storm lasts forever," Sir Gyzmo had wisely advised.

"But I miss her so much!" Willow sobbed.

"You must honor the memory of your mother, Willow. Polish your fondest memories of her as if they were gold, then place them on the shelf of your heart to cherish, knowing that you can reach for them at any time you like and experience those moments once again," Sir Gyzmo had whispered.

Sir Gyzmo had spoken the truth, and the pair's journeys had been guided by faith. Eventually, Willow's heart healed, and she was able to step into the future she was destined to live—becoming a heroine with her canine hero always by her side.

Deception

Lately, Wynter had been feeling less and less like the woman she once was and more and more like the woman she did not want to be. Once upon a time, she had been considered a fair-haired beauty who possessed a pure and kind heart. She was a human born in Snowdonia, an ancient valley carved from ice, where dragons are known to sleep, and magic is everywhere. It was during the shiver season of winter that Wynter arrived in this world as the full Cold moon glowed radiantly in the sky.

She possessed snow-colored hair and icy blue eyes. She was so lightweight and graceful that she seemed to float slightly above the ground when she walked. She had a quiet, hypnotic voice that was as spellbinding as watching falling snowflakes. She exuded a goodness that others were drawn to like a magnet, and the sheepherder known as Aidan was no exception. He was awe-struck when he met Wynter in the Crooked Forest, and he sought after her affection instantly.

It had begun as an uneventful day. Aidan was searching for a water source for his flock of sheep as he did most days. He was lost in his own thoughts, contemplating which course to try next, when he first laid eyes on her.

She was immaculately dressed, wearing a bright purple hooded cloak that highlighted her alabaster skin. The garment was clasped in place at the neck with a bronze and garnet broach that marked her regal status. Snow-white curls escaped from around her hood, framing her face. Mesmerized, Aidan found himself approaching the beauty. She smiled at the wayward sheepherder as he approached. With his work worn hands, Aidan reached toward Wynter, grasping a single silky blonde curl, twisting the silky tuft with his fingers as if he had known her forever.

Wynter's smile broadened as she watched him. "I'm Wynter," she said introducing herself. "You are quite bold, sir."

The words hung in the air for a moment before Aidan snapped out of his trance, releasing the curl and finding his voice.

Clearing his throat before speaking, he stuttered, "Morning, Miss, I'm Aidan. Please don't be upset with me for saying that you are the most beautiful being I have ever seen. You will have to forgive me for I have been completely captivated by your presence. How is it that our paths have never crossed before?"

"I couldn't say. I'm just on my way to New Leaf," Wynter smiled, feeling oddly comfortable with the stranger.

"New Leaf?" Aidan questioned. "I've lived in this forest all my life and I have never heard of the place."

"It's a new town. I'm considering making a home there. I once lived just along the edge of the loveliest little village called Flowerville. I was forced to leave there due to drought. Some of the townspeople of Flowerville are forming a town called New Leaf, meaning to start over and live in a different manner."

"I see," Aidan muttered, shifting awkwardly from one foot to another.

"There was a man that lived near Flowerville," Wynter continued. "I never met him, but it is said that he had no respect for nature or the elemental beings. Due to his reckless behavior, we all suffered. He cost us Dragonfly Ditch, our precious water source. Can you imagine such a person with this type of personality?"

Aidan's heart skipped a beat as he stared at the beautiful Wynter. He felt the fleeting opportunity to speak the truth and admit the error of his ways to Wynter, letting her know that he was the one she spoke of. But he was not that brave.

"No, Miss, I don't believe I can imagine such a person," Aidan lied. And that is precisely when the trouble between Wynter and Aidan began.

"It was heartbreaking to leave my home in Flowerville behind. But I am trying to begin anew," Wynter said.

"Maybe you could show me this place called New Leaf," Aidan asked. "I would love to see it."

Wynter smiled as the two walked side by side through the forest until the village was visible.

"There," Wynter pointed to a hillside dotted with new huts. But Aidan was looking at Wynter more than at New Leaf. He must find a way to get to know her better.

In the days to come, the pair spent more and more time together, and it felt like the most natural thing in the world that they would marry. And so it came to pass that one sunshiny day, Aidan and Wynter observed the custom of their time, by joining hands, and began their wedding ceremony by drawing an invisible circle around themselves as a sign of their unity. The bride wore a tartan-colored sash pinned to her shoulder. Her stunning broach holding the fabric in place. In a sachet, she carried yarrow as a love charm, and she carried a bouquet of lavender that symbolized the loyalty and devotion she felt for Aidan.

Aidan was a handsome yet nervous groom. He had insisted on a private ceremony away from the townsfolk. After the ceremony, the couple retreated to their new home, where they began their life together. Wynter had high hopes for her new life, but her home soon became lonely, as Aidan was mostly gone, off grazing and tending his sheep and searching for new water sources. When he was home, he insisted they stay to themselves and away from their neighbors' watchful eyes.

During one of Aidan's recent absences, Wynter had been tending her vegetable garden when she accidentally overheard some whisperings from two women from the village talking about Wynter's new husband and his identity. It was suspected that he might be the very person that was responsible for the drought in Flowerville and the one who had angered the elemental fairy, Dewdrop. This was the beginning of the subtle, uncomfortable fluttering's that began inside of Wynter's heart.

Upon Aidan's return, Wynter questioned him outright about his previous life before they had met, but Aidan's answers were steeped in mystery and were unclear and vague. As the months passed, the cycle of lies became difficult for Aidan to keep track of, and he began to act defensively, often lashing out at Wynter, shifting the attention away from himself and onto her. Months turned to years, and it was with great regret that Wynter realized she had been deprived of an honest picture of the man she had chosen to marry.

The honeymoon phase of Wynter's marriage was over. She was tired of living mostly alone with a man whom she didn't understand. She could not imagine a life without Aidan, but Aidan's secrets and lies had jeopardized Wynter's trust and damaged the relationship irreparably, leaving Wynter feeling that she had married a stranger.

So Wynter left the marriage home. It was neither planned nor predicted. She simply whisked her purple cloak from the hook where it hung by the door, and off she went, with no plot or destination. By the time Willow and Sir Gyzmo discovered the pure-hearted beauty, it appeared to be too late, as a considerable amount of time had passed since the day of her sudden departure. She was now hardly recognizable as the same woman. She had lost far too much weight, as food no longer interested her. Her beautiful blue eyes had become swollen and puffy from the tears she wept over the man she loved and his inability to be truthful. She was literary slipping away when Sir Gyzmo and Willow discovered her thin, lifeless body lying on an ancient stone beside the sacred well.

Queen of Spring, we honor you
On this special day
As the leaves turn green
And the flowers bloom
We pay tribute to your name
It is now the time
To plant our seeds
All along our way
As we ask for fairy blessings
On this joyful Beltane day.

Beltane

It was the beginning of the month of May, or the cross-quarter day called Beltane, the exact mid-point between the spring equinox and the summer solstice. New life was bursting out everywhere, and it was clear that the wheel of nature had turned. The days had become noticeably longer and warmer. New life was beginning to emerge, and the earth was being reborn again.

This day held a special magic because the veil between the present world and the otherworld was considered thin enough to cross. It was a time for honoring fairies and tree spirits and their magical energy.

Some of the townsfolk of New Leaf had risen at first light of dawn to gather flowers and branches from the Crooked Forest to decorate their homes and the sacred places like wells, fairy forts, and springs to please and honor the nature spirits.

Beltane means bright fire, and Aidan knew that he should practice the ritual designed to protect his flock of sheep and encourage their growth during the upcoming season. Since his encounter with Dewdrop, he wasn't about to take another chance disrespecting the nature spirits.

He would light a special Beltane bonfire this morning, then drive his herd through the smoke. He would then gather a small number of embers from the sacred fire and take them to his home to light the evening fire there to not only warm his cold and lonely home, but also in hopes of appeasing the nature spirits and asking them to aid in the return of his missing wife.

May Fae

May Fae recognized that from water life emerges, making water the most significant of the elements. The sacred well she was bound to percolated out of the earth from the unseen realm called the Otherworld. This was May Fae's power center. It was custom that those seeking answers to the problems that plagued them often visited the well and would linger there for some time to contact the fairy mistress known as May Fae. It was common knowledge that the well was the best place to get in touch with her mysticism, particularly on Beltane Day when the veil is thin.

May Fae was a magical creature who possessed the ability to fly and make flowers bloom at her will. It was said she could conjure gold, and some even said that she glowed in the dark. The truth was that May Fae could cast charms for any situation, and curses that could last for hundreds of years.

Wynter had lost track of how many days she had been rambling through the woods. She was in a declining state and couldn't continue in this way much longer. She needed help. Wynter knew that May Fae resided at the sacred well, and she found herself instinctively traveling toward it so she could ask the fairy mistress for advice regarding her predicament.

At the wells entrance, the crooked pine trees grew dense and thick, bent at their bases, acting as guardians, and shielding access, making the sacred well mostly unseen to the casual observer. A large ancient stone sat beside the well, offering a seat for weary travelers to rest.

Wynter entered and circled the well sunwise, or in a clockwise direction, knowing that circling to the left was considered taboo. Reaching for her most elegant possession, her bronze and garnet broach, she unfastened the gem and flung it into the well in the spirit of giving and to show respect and honor to May Fae. Lying down upon the ancient stone, she mysteriously became drowsy as if she had taken a potion as she focused her thoughts to summon the water fairy.

Hearing Wynter's thoughts, May Fae awakened from deep within the mysterious depths of the well. Her beauty was staggering. She possessed nine thick, heavy golden braids, laced with pink flowers that spun and swirled around her body. Her large brown eyes were filled with empathy as she observed Wynter's distressed and worn body lying upon the ancient stone. In her long, elegant fingers, she held Wynter's precious broach, which she softly laid into Wynter's outstretched hand.

"Keep this with you," she spoke before singing her magical fairy song that cast a spell over all those who heard it, making them want to stay and hear the melody for as long as they could.

My gift to you is filled with love
My song as soothing as a dove
When I appear, I will bestow
The answers for the way to go
Listen carefully before you start
My song can heal your troubled heart

As May Fae sang, she compassionately placed her palm on Wynter's forehead, and this is what she heard:

I picked a flower in my dreams
It was beautiful to see
But when I woke, I realized
There were no blooms for me
There was a star once in my life
But his light no longer shines
Our love has passed
And slipped away
Into another time

"You do not have to carry this burden alone," May Fae gently whispered to Wynter. "I am here for good reason, to help you. Your diminishing condition will not be easy to vanquish if it is possible at all, my dear."

"Stay in the light. That is the direct opposite of the darkness you are feeling. I am here to act as your guide. I possess the wisdom of the old traditions and I am ready to transfer this knowledge to you," Mae Fae whispered ever so lightly in Wynter's ear.

"How could I have made such a foolish mistake in the choice of a husband? He should have told me who he was!" Wynter silently conveyed.

"You must put aside your hearts yearnings for what might have been and know that there is a season and a reason for every life experience. You entwined your heart with another human being, dear girl, there is no shame in that," Mae Fae wisely advised.

"But I loved him!" Wynter winced.

"You loved the man that he showed you, my dear, and not the man he truly is. The question you must now ask yourself is, now that you know who he is, can you continue to love him?" Mae Fae questioned.

A single tear fell from the corner of Wynter's eye.

"It's a tragedy, Wynter. But only you can decide where you go from here. Life changes by the second, never to be the same as it was again. Don't lose faith. You are strong enough to overcome the pain you are feeling and find forgiveness in your heart for Aidan," May Fae whispered.

"What should I do?" Wynter stirred from her trance like state, seeing the fairy mistress standing over her for only an instant before May Fae's image faded.

"It is time for you to embark upon a journey for a destination that holds a special place in your heart. Trust your intuition to know where that place is. When you arrive there, it will be your mission to gather herbs and plants of the earth during certain seasons throughout the days, and hours for the next year and one day."

"You will devote yourself to this task daily and you will add the gathered ingredients to the boiling water of the magical cauldron that awaits your arrival at your destination. After one year and one day have passed, you will drink from the brew you have created. By then, you will have come to know the lessons of forgiveness, and the answer to the question that troubles your heart. Then you will be prepared to start anew," May Fae conveyed before vanishing back into her elemental home, and Wynter fell deeply asleep—her weary body slumped next to the sacred well.

A Fairy Song

During their adventures together, Willow and Sir Gyzmo trekked great distances within the mystical Crooked Forest. They learned to sit quietly when arriving in a new landscape, breathing in the smells of the ancient old growth forest and sensing the rhythm of the earth, the wind, and all the living things. They focused their attention to the earth, the sky, and the movements of the breeze through the branches. And, in return, the landscape literally settled in around them, accepting them as life carried on, remaining undisturbed.

They marked time by counting days from sunset to sunset; and when the moon was full, they would walk at night, as the gravitational pull of the full moon lessened the effect of gravity, and they could conserve energy.

Their knowledge of the natural world aided them in navigating the ancient trackway system woven throughout the forest.

On this May morning, Sir Gyzmo and Willow were harvesting grapevine and shaping it to craft a special Beltane wreath. Willow had picked fresh myrtle to weave throughout the vine, as flower lore says myrtle is home to the earth elementals who open the buds of plants in the spring and care for all growing things in general.

Sir Gyzmo buried his nose inside the fragrant evergreen shrub that was covered with small, glossy green leaves and white star-shaped flowers, filling his lungs with the myrtle's warm aroma.

Unexpectedly he stopped, lifting his nose from the sweet-smelling blooms as a song emanated from the hills and knolls before him. It was as if a spell had been cast over the fairy dog and Willow too, as they heard a tune, not of this world—it was so sweet in nature. It was the finest, grandest, and most beautiful song that they had ever heard. There was the sound of bells mixed with the exquisite, amazing richness of a female voice singing a melody in slow moving waves that seemed to hypnotize the pair.

"Do you think it could be May Fae?" Willow breathlessly asked Sir Gyzmo

"We are close to her sacred well," Sir Gyzmo responded.

Drawn to the mystical tune; the pair traveled toward the music, hypnotized by the sound.

Neither asked "Is it real?" Instead, they trusted that there must be a significance that they heard the song at all, as they had no problem shifting between the magic of the moment and the reality of everyday life.

The melodious, angelic tune led them to the desired destination as they carried their wreath, just as others in the vicinity had carried petals and branches to decorate the sacred places like May Fae's well on this first day of May.

Upon their arrival, Sir Gyzmo and Willow were astonished to find the limp and lifeless looking body of the beautiful Wynter slumped against the stone that offered rest for those that travelled to May Fae's well, seeking answers for the problems they faced.

Awake

Wynter felt as if she had been asleep for one hundred years. The mystic, mournful rhythm of May Fae's song had touched the deepest chords of her soul.

Squinting her eyes, she struggled to sit up. *"Just how long have I been here?"* she thought to herself. Looking beside her, she saw fresh bouquets and branches and petals entwined with ribbon, all left as an offering to the elemental world on this beautiful Beltane morning.

"It's still Beltane," Wynter whispered to herself, feeling relieved.

Sir Gyzmo carefully nudged Wynter's lifeless hand with his nose, and Wynter turned her head to gaze upon the valiant fairy dog and Willow, who stood at his side.

"Easy does it," Willow instructed as she coaxed the beautiful Wynter into sitting up.

Wynter glanced around getting her bearings. "I am so tired," She whispered

"Don't worry, Miss, we will take care of you," Willow stated

"Why are you here?" Wynter questioned.

"Sir Gyzmo and I heard the song of May Fae, and it would have been a dishonor to her to have ignored it, so we followed the tune here to the scared well, and now I see why we were guided here," Willow calmly stated.

"I came here in search of answers for my broken heart, thinking surely May Fae could help me. But the whole experience was confusing," Wynter said as her fingers embraced the broach that she remembered throwing into the well.

"You saw her?" Sir Gyzmo questioned.

"Oh, yes. I saw her. She left me with a message. I am to embark upon a mission. But I am confused as to what I am to do when I arrive at my destination," Wynter said.

"What did she instruct you to do?" Sir Gyzmo asked.

"I am to gather certain herbs and plants of the earth during certain seasons, days, and hours for the next year and one day. Then I must boil the ingredients in the magical cauldron that awaits my arrival. At the end of one year and one day, I am to drink the potion I have created, and only then will I know what to do about this grave situation in which I find myself," Wynter answered.

Sir Gyzmo and Willow looked at each other before looking back at Wynter. She was appearing to come to life before their eyes. The color was returning to her cheeks, and her ice blue eyes were becoming clearer.

"Do you know of this ritual?" Wynter questioned Willow

"Yes. My mother taught me about plants and herbs before we were separated. As Shuns, we are considered keepers of the forests, so it's only natural for us to recognize the medicinal and nutritional value of all Mother Earth provides and what seasons those remedies are accessible," Willow answered.

"Do you think you could educate me about plants and herbs and how they are used and when they come into season?" Wynter inquired. "Any knowledge that you could pass on to me would be greatly appreciated. I am afraid I can't say that I have the same understanding of nature as you do."

"I am sure Willow would be happy to teach you," Sir Gyzmo began. "But that might take a considerable amount of time. It's not something that one can fully comprehend in just a day."

"Perfect!" Wynter said, rising to her feet and dusting off her clothes. "I will be returning to Snowdonia, my birthplace, to perform the ritual, so you can both accompany me. I would love your company and Willow can teach me along the way."

Willow and Sir Gyzmo glanced knowingly at each. They had been guided here to this place and time for a reason. Otherwise, this experience would not be presenting itself to them.

"We are happy to travel along with you, and I will teach you about the natural world along the way," Willow answered. "But before we depart, we must leave our Beltane wreath beside the well to pay honor to May Fae."

As Sir Gyzmo and Willow laid their Beltane wreath made from myrtle flowers beside May Fae's well, they gave thanks that they had been guided here to assist the distressed and weary Wynter, who obviously needed their help so much.

"We go!" Sir Gyzmo instructed after giving thanks to May Fae, as a true hero would, and the journey began.

Snowdonia

Just as May Fae had advised, Wynter instinctively knew that returning to her birthplace of Snowdonia to perform the ritual was the right thing to do. The journey took weeks, and all along the way, Willow shared her knowledge of the natural world with Wynter.

She taught her about the simple beauty and awe-inspiring hardiness and strength of snowdrop flowers and how they herald the beginning of spring. She taught her about wild garlic as they passed a carpet of wide green leaves that adorned the woodlands and how those tiny healing oil infused bulbs produce a delicate herb with white fragrant flowers and a strong pungent aroma. She showed her how to make a glorious tea from the dazzling yellow flowers of the dandelion and how to crush acorns, the fruit of the oak tree, so that they could be added to the brew.

Upon their arrival in Snowdonia, Sir Gyzmo and Willow were struck by the silence and stillness of the place. There was heaviness in the air, not in an oppressive manner, but in a manner that reflected the magic and the wisdom of the region.

Their noses were enticed by the aroma of the abundant herbs and wildflowers that grew here naturally. Alchemilla, meadowsweet, coltsfoot, honeysuckle, and bramble grew prolifically here, providing ample ingredients for the brewing of the potion that Wynter would create over the next one year and one day.

"There it is!" Sir Gyzmo pointed toward a shimmering cauldron cast from the finest iron, the likes of which were rarely seen. Just as May Fae had predicted, the magical cauldron awaited Wynter's arrival.

Willow looked wistfully at Wynter. She would miss the friend she had grown so close to during the time they had spent together.

"It's time for you to begin," Willow sighed. "Sir Gyzmo and I will miss you, my friend, but your future awaits."

Wynter glanced at the cauldron, then back to her friends. "I will miss you both as well. But I must confess, I am a little afraid. I'm not as brave as you are Willow."

"Oh, you are, my dear, you just don't know it yet," Willow replied, taking Wynter's hand in hers.

"We wish you well!" Sir Gyzmo said wistfully, knowing that it was quite possible that he might never see his new friend again.

"You have been well instructed on our journey together on which herbs and plants you will need and when. See this through to the end," Willow said as she departed.

Waving goodbye to Sir Gyzmo and Willow, Wynter felt a sinking feeling in her heart. What had she done coming all this way to embark upon such a tedious process of healing?

Turning back toward the cauldron, she realized she had no other choice. As Willow had said, it was time for her to begin. Gathering dead limbs and branches, she built a fire under the cauldron's belly and filled the pot with water from nearby Lake Ogwen. It was day one. She was to gather myrtle, the first plant required for the ritual. As she added the myrtle blossoms to the boiling pot, she prayed. The flames from the fire licked the cauldrons' belly, warming the brew and the one who sat beside the simmering pot, hoping for better days ahead.

The Crossroads

As the day's passed, Wynter gathered the sacred herbs, roots, and flowers and cast them into the cauldron, the magic rising with the addition of every ingredient. She did not take this task lightly, dedicating a year and one day of her life took utter commitment. The journey to heal herself proved to be difficult, one that a coward would never be brave enough to embark upon. But Wynter had faith that she could access the mystery of the cauldron. She would visualize that final day of her commitment when she would drink the brew that was only meant for her, and she would be granted the wisdom to know the direction she must take in her life. Stirring the cauldron, Wynter added elder and pine needles, speaking these words:

> My heart is broken
> My pain is deep
> Because the truth
> He could not keep

May Fae had wisely instructed Wynter, knowing that she needed time to heal and sort through and grieve the loss she felt. The purpose of the yearlong ritual was to immerse Wynter totally in the experience without distraction. The intention of the rite was to connect via the powers of nature, enabling Wynter to question, ponder, and conclude her transformation.

And as the month's passed, the collected range of ingredients were continually brewed over a low heat in the cauldron, then set aside and added to the previous month's brew. Upon that final day of tending the brew, Wynter drank the concoction she had created.

Gazing at the cauldron, she watched as the final embers burned under its warm belly. Rising from her seat, she made ready to embark back to the place where the two roads crossed. The same place she had arrived over a year ago with Sir Gyzmo and Willow. Placing her bright purple cloak around her shoulders, she clasped the garment around her neck, fastening the hand-hammered bronze and garnet broach in place, starting toward the crossroads.

She had not spoken to another living being in a very long time. Her time in Snowdonia would remain private. She chose not to speak of what had occurred within herself during the last one year and one day, as the experience would only make sense to the one immersed in the experience.

Arriving at the crossroads, at the betwixt and between place, Wynter felt lighter. Here, there were no rules or obligations, even the marriage law was suspended here. She was free to do as she pleased.

Which road would she take? One road led back to the Crooked Forest. Wynter smiled as she thought of her friends, Sir Gyzmo and Willow. She wondered how they were and if she might locate them again in the forest. The other road led to the village of New Leaf where she and Aidan had made their marriage home. What did their future together hold?

The cauldron had brewed its magic. Wynter knew that the end of this tale was merely the beginning of another, and she was ready to initiate the next phase of her life journey.

The air felt exceptionally hot and humid for this time of year, and the wind began to pick up as Wynter took the first steps into her new reality.

Cloud-Crazed

Willow had been taught by a wise old woman how to read the clouds for messages. Over time, she developed an intense understanding of the clouds and the combinations of clouds that shared the sky. She had learned that clouds provide clues about what is likely to occur as the day progresses. She observed the clouds to decipher messages and impending weather patterns. She learned that the speed in which the clouds move can indicate how fast events will come to pass or how long it will take before the event dissipates. The sky is in a constant flux of growth and change, just like life, so Willow was keenly aware of the sky throughout the course of the day.

"You are cloud-crazed!" Sir Gyzmo chuckled.

"I know." Willow laughed. "But I've learned how important it is to pay attention to nature's messages.

"And what do the clouds tell you about today?" Sir Gyzmo questioned.

Willow glanced up at the sky, pointing toward a yellow-colored cloud. "Be patient and strong, there are obstacles to come," Willow answered.

There were thunderclouds brewing overhead, and the edges were becoming sharper and the color was darker, indicating that the clouds contained power.

"The clouds are becoming darker and larger. We should expect a squall within a few hours," Willow advised.

Sir Gyzmo felt the fur on his back begin to rise as he stared up toward the horizon, and a gust of heavy wind hinted at a sudden change in the weather.

Derecho

While most storms can be heard approaching from several miles away, this storm attacked unexpectedly and without warning, making it even more treacherous due to its relative silence.

Willow and Sir Gyzmo sensed the power of the storm just seconds before it struck. Sand and grit carried by blasts of air ripped through the forest, scouring everything in its path as the eerie yellow clouds grew and spread across the entire sky. The hot humid air had created a somewhat rare weather event known as a derecho, which had traveled along a straight swath through the Crooked Forest.

As the treacherous winds gusted, searching for shelter was the first thing that came to Willow and Sir Gyzmo's mind, but where? Low visibility disoriented them as they fought against the blowing wind.

Just ahead, Sir Gyzmo spied an open entryway that led into a stone hut structure. That would be a good place to ride out the storm, if they could only make it to the doorway as they fought against the violent winds.

Pickletoe

Pickletoe was a stone troll. He was regarded by most in the Crooked Forest as grotesque and even hideous. Standing only two feet tall with a huge potbelly, he had grayish skin, a broad mouth, and strong jaws. His large, long nose was covered with warts and twigs grew from his green shaggy hair. His long green tail twitched from side to side as he navigated his route by tuning into the vibration that emanated from under his large feet and even larger toes as he traveled in quest of enough food to fulfill his massive appetite and file down his flat teeth that grew continuously and at a fast rate.

Pickletoe lived in an ancient stone hut that sheltered him from sunlight during the day. When exposed to daylight, stone trolls turn back into the stone they were born from. And if there were any who fail to believe in such a fairy tale, the evidence of this legend was visible from Pickletoe's hut.

The stone cliffs directly behind his hut were referred to as the Troll Mountains. Legend said that the stone trolls alive in this area had been caught out past sunrise, and as is their fate, turned to stone instantly when exposed to the morning sunlight. Their three faces were visible in between the crevices and crags of the Troll Mountains.

Pickletoe made sure that he didn't meet the same fate as his three brothers had. During the day, he slept on a bed made from grasses and leaves, tucked safely inside his troll home, and shielded from the devastating sunlight. Only under cover of darkness did he dare leave his home in search of nourishment.

As added protection, Pickletoe carved a sundial from stone. The time-measuring device was just outside the entry of his stone hut, pointing toward the North Star, keeping the troll mindful of the remaining sunlight of the day.

With the birth of the village of New Leaf, life had become increasingly difficult for the trolls. Before New Leaf, there had not been any humans near the Troll Mountains for over fifty miles in all directions.

But lately, the forest was filled with the sounds of cutting and sawing as new settlers arrived, clearing their own personal patch within the Crooked Forest.

Food had become scarce as well. Now Pickletoe had to share the forest's bounty with the humans who were seeking game for their growing families. The addition of humans had also added an element of danger that wasn't previously there. Now, Pickletoe had to watch out for traps and snares that the villagers had set to collect game. He had recently had a close call with a fox trap by getting too close to the trap and nearly losing his tail.

But Pickletoe remained on Troll Mountain. After all, he had lived there for the past three thousand years. He loved his turtle-shaped stone hut with the triangular front entry that he had carefully constructed to be in perfect alignment with the winter solstice sunset.

Pickletoe had been the strongest of all his brothers; therefore, they had crowned him as a troll king and always followed his orders. But his brothers were now forever frozen in stone, and the other trolls in the Crooked Forest did not possess the same tolerance for the troll king's ego as his blood brothers had.

Pickletoe considered himself handsome. He was strong and healthy, and his large toes that resembled pickles were a great trait for providing and for troll survival. He believed he would make an excellent companion, but any prospective sweethearts that he met avoided him at every turn.

The absence of his brothers added to his loneliness. Mostly he stayed home, guarding the thousand-year fire burning in his hearth that kept it warm inside his stone hut.

Nestled in his cozy bed on this springtime afternoon, his sleep was abruptly interrupted by a sudden straight-line wind that blew through the front door of his hut, rustling his green fur and startling the troll awake during the middle of the day when anyone knows that stone trolls should be sound asleep.

Potatoes, Eggs, and Tea Leaves

Through the entry hole of his stone hut, Pickletoe witnessed the shattered branches, leaves, dirt, and sand blowing past his home. He felt the grit of the sand in his long, sharp teeth, and the nonstop, thunderous sound of the wind filled his large hairy ears, frightening him, even though he was a stone troll.

Pickletoe held on to his bed tightly. His long gray fingers gripping the edge of his bed as if they could hold him in place and keep him from blowing away. The wind abruptly shifted in direction and a swift gust blew through the front door, landing Sir Gyzmo and Willow who were only a few feet away from the stone troll, seated in a pile of leaves, dust, and dirt, looking just as confused as Pickletoe felt.

Willow and Sir Gyzmo were frozen in place, staring at Pickletoe, then at each other. Trolls were known for their unpredictable behavior, so they knew to proceed cautiously. For all they knew, Pickletoe could see the two of them as his next meal. Some fast thinking was required.

"Good day," Sir Gyzmo finally found his voice. "I hope you don't mind the intrusion. The wind blew us in."

"We mean no harm, sir," Willow cautiously stated.

Pickletoe narrowed his eyes, studying the pair. They were small, but they could make a nice light snack for a very hungry troll.

Willow seemed to read the trolls mind as she carefully reached for her knapsack.

"We are most happy to share our food with you," Willow smartly offered.

The stone trolls' eyes focused on the bulging knapsack, and he felt curious as to its contents. He could certainly use a good meal. Maybe he could tolerate this abrupt invasion of his privacy if there was something in it for him.

Generally, Pickletoe would do all his hunting at night, after sunset, safe from being turned to stone, but this storm was going to keep him from accomplishing this basic task.

"Do you have pots to cook in?" Sir Gyzmo inquired.

"Ugh!" Pickletoe grumbled as he trudged over to the corner of his troll home, sorting through his grinding stones and fetching a large cauldron and two smaller kettles that he normally used to cook his meals.

"Will these do?" Pickletoe questioned, raising one hairy eyebrow.

"They are perfect," Sir Gyzmo responded.

Adding water to all three pots, Pickletoe positioned each kettle over his low-burning fire.

"I have potatoes, eggs, and tea leaves," Willow stated, removing each item from her knapsack.

Pickletoe eyed the food hungrily, saliva dripping from his enormous jowls.

"By the way, we haven't introduced ourselves," Willow stated. "I'm Willow, and this is Sir Gyzmo, my enchanted fairy dog."

Pickletoe rubbed his hairy chin. He had heard the stories of Sir Gyzmo and Willow that had been circulating within the Crooked Forest. They were known for their wisdom, and their adventures were infamous. This changed everything. Maybe they could advise him regarding the romantic troubles that plagued him.

Pickletoe was three thousand years old, and it was time to begin thinking about finding a companion. These days, the troll women he knew turned away from him when they saw him approach, and he wasn't quite sure why. Surely, they found him handsome. Surely, they found him intelligent. Why, at every opportunity that he was given, he voiced these opinions quite boisterously.

"What should I do?" Pickletoe asked Willow. "The other trolls avoid me and don't respect my status as the king of trolls. I am lonely and would like a companion, but rarely do I encounter another of my kind, and when I do, I think they dodge me and duck away to hide. Maybe I should be louder and more forceful when I speak with them, or maybe I should be subtle and quieter. I'm just not sure. I'm certainly handsome enough and smart enough to attract a mate." Pickletoe grinned showing his long sharp teeth.

Willow smiled back at the troll. "Let me help you find a solution to your dilemma."

"Place these potatoes, eggs, and tea leaves in the boiling water of each separate pot and keep an eye on them until they are done," Willow quietly advised.

Pickletoe had no idea what any of this had to do with his lack of companionship, but he obliged due to his enormous appetite, watching the pots until enough time had passed for each item to be thoroughly cooked.

"Peel the eggs, peel the potatoes, and strain the tea leaves," Willow instructed.

Pickletoe was confused, but he did as he was told and filled three plates and three bowls for each of them as they sat down together to enjoy their meal.

"Notice how each of these items was placed in the boiling water for the same amount of time, yet each responded to the boiling water differently," Willow stated.

"Whatever are you talking about?" Pickletoe asked, more confused than ever, staring at his plate of food and his bowl full of tea.

"The egg was soft but now it's hard. The potato was hard, but now it is soft. The tea leaves have changed the water itself," Willow quietly stated.

Pickletoe looked blankly at his plate, not seeing any significance at all between the cooked food and his problems.

"I don't understand what any of this has to do with me!" the troll stammered.

"When problems come up and we find ourselves in hot water, we must learn to react in the correct manner."

Pickletoe moved the food around on his plate, then sipped tea from his bowl as he contemplated the meaning of the lesson.

"I don't understand how any of this applies to my love life," Pickletoe stated shaking his head from side to side.

"There is a lesson here, Pickletoe. Listen carefully. When placed in boiling water, the potato that was hard and strong before it was boiled becomes soft and, if dropped, will turn to mush. The fragile, delicate egg when boiled hardens on the inside. The tea leaves were unique. They changed the boiling water itself, giving it a savory flavor and aroma. The tea leaves created something entirely new."

"If you want to change your current situation you will need to be like the tea leaves that changed the water, not like the potato that was too soft or the egg that became too hard. You should consider changing the approach you use.

"You don't need to be loud and boisterous to attract a mate, nor do you need to be so soft that you might be taken advantage of. You are far more likely to attract a mate that is your equal by just being your true self. No pretenses are necessary," Willow instructed.

"You are a smart one," Pickletoe finally said, smiling the tiniest of smiles. "It's true what they say about you. You are very wise."

"I can't take credit for this lesson, Pickletoe. It is an old story taught to me by my mother," Willow wistfully remembered.

Silence then fell upon the trio as they enjoyed their dinner safe and warm inside the troll hut.

Bloom

Bloom was an elemental earth fairy and the magical gardener of nature in the Crooked Forest. She was born from a flower seed, and just like Mother Earth whom she protected, she was stable, nurturing, and firm. She knew that everything in nature was endowed with spirit and intelligence, and that every blossom holds information deposited by birds and bees.

Bloom represented the life phases of birth, death, and rebirth. She arrived from the north, born at precisely midnight during the season of winter, taking refuge inside a crooked pine tree. She was green and brown in color like the earth, and wildflowers grew from her fingertips, and green vines encircled her body.

The Otherworld was Bloom's domain. There she remained hidden from mortal eyes.

"What we do to the earth, we do to ourselves" was her mantra. She cherished those who possessed sincerity and a natural childlike innocence like Luna, and to those she would bestow assistance and protection.

Luna had not realized that on that tragic day, when Aidan pursued her for miles through the forest, that she was not alone. Bloom had been there, and she had felt Luna's distress. She knew that Luna was too weak to locate her precious daughter, so she watched over her. On that first night when Luna made refuge inside a small tree hole in an ancient, crooked pine, Bloom was with her. The next morning, Bloom walked beside Luna while the earth trembled and shook, and Luna fell backward, becoming suspended in a place where time was no longer measured.

"This is where time begins and ends," Bloom had guided Luna.

Luna had healed while in a suspended state, but now it was time for her to return to the Crooked Forest, to that very same location where she had abruptly departed quite some time ago. Luna's consciousness stirred, and she heard Bloom's message, yet there was no visible source for the sound.

"Any plant disconnected from its roots will wither and die. Remain rooted and grounded in the earth's power to flourish. It is time for you to return to the person you are meant to be and the life you are destined to live," Bloom murmured. "Breathe in the light, Luna, the time has come for your return."

Luna felt herself land back in the Crooked Forest. She was slightly nauseous, and her legs were wobbly and unsteady from her ascension out of the Otherworld.

As she gained her bearings, the high-pitched sound of an eagle crying out could be heard overhead. One single downy under feather from the eagle's belly floated gently down to earth, landing directly in Luna's path. Luna understood instantly this was no accident. She knew the feather was meant for her.

Luna picked up the feather then walked over to a nearby juniper tree, tying the feather to a limb. She whispered this prayer and gifted the feather back to Mother Earth:

> Daughter Willow, come to me
> As I speak your name
> I know you cannot see me
> But I call out just the same
> Hear my voice, dear daughter
> As I journey back to you
> Feel my distant heartbeat
> From my heart that is so blue

The winds wafted over the eagle feather, sending a pulsating vibration through the universe as Luna's prayer was heard.

The Voice

The derecho had lasted for nine consecutive days. Hurricane force winds, tornadoes, heavy rain, hail, and flash flooding had occurred, wreaking havoc and devastation, especially in the newly founded town of New Leaf.

On the evening of the ninth night, Willow laid her weary head upon her knapsack, tucked in securely beside Sir Gyzmo's gentle sleeping form, safe and secure inside Pickletoe's stone hut. In those first moments of restful sleep, her heart skipped a beat when out of nowhere she heard her name being called quite clearly and quite urgently, yet the source of the voice was unclear.

"Willow!" the voice called a second time, even louder this time.

Willow sat up quite suddenly, looking around to determine where the voice was coming from. Sir Gyzmo awoke and Pickletoe snored loudly upon his cozy cot of leaves and grasses in front of his ancient fire.

"Is something wrong?" Sir Gyzmo gently inquired of his beloved Willow. "You seem as if you have seen a ghost."

"She's alive!" Willow exclaimed loudly, waking the stone troll from his slumber.

"Who's alive?" Pickletoe questioned, rubbing sleep from his eyes and placing his large feet firmly upon the floor ready to take any action required.

"My mother!" Willow cried. "She's alive!"

Pickletoe looked around his stone hut as if another Shun could suddenly appear just as suddenly as Sir Gyzmo and Willow had blown through his front door that very first day of the storm.

"Where is she? I don't see her," Pickletoe said, turning his head in all directions, surveying the corners of his hut as if she might materialize anywhere.

"We have to go!" Willow said to Sir Gyzmo as she gathered their meager belongings, stuffing them into her knapsack.

"I trust you know where we are traveling to," Sir Gyzmo said ready to embark upon this unplanned journey.

"I do!" Willow responded confidently.

"Thank you so much, Pickletoe, for sheltering us through this terrible storm," Willow spoke.

An unexpected tear formed in the corner of the stone troll's eye, and he quickly brushed it away, realizing that he would miss his uninvited guests. They had taught him much during their time together, and he felt far more confident about his ability to find a mate based on the lessons he had learned.

"I'm not exactly sure I want you to go," Pickletoe found himself saying. "I have enjoyed your company so much. I'm not sure I want to live alone again."

"Remember the lessons learned, dear Pickletoe, and you won't be alone for long. After all, you are a handsome and intelligent stone troll, one that would be a fine companion for the right mate." Willow smiled.

As they stepped out into the moonlit night, Willow looked up into the stars with confidence. She instinctively knew where Luna was and that she was safe and sound and waiting for her daughter to return. Sir Gyzmo stood at Willow's side knowing he would follow her anywhere without question.

"Farewell, my friend," Willow spoke as she hugged Pickletoe goodbye.

"Blessings be with you," Sir Gyzmo said to Pickletoe, knowing once more that he might never see his new friend again.

As Pickletoe stood outside his ancient hut, he felt sad that his new friends were leaving. They would be missed. But he also felt happy knowing that his newfound confidence and understanding would aid him in the quest of a companion.

Glancing at his finely crafted ancient sundial, he was reminded of time and that many hours remained before the light of dawn. The storm had passed, and it was time to resume his regular routine of hunting at night before the light of day crept over the Troll Mountains.

Devastation

~⁑ ⁑~

It was the time of the Fairy Moon of May. The primitive roadways throughout the Crooked Forest were illuminated by the romantic charm of the moon's rays, and the crooked pines shined brightly. Sir Gyzmo and Willow strolled toward their destination, feeling as though they were wide-awake within a most pleasurable dream.

Willow's past problems and worries dissipated, and she was filled with joy and renewed energy and strength. It was a thrilling and enchanting experience to know that Luna was safe and awaiting her arrival.

"I feel as if we are nearly floating above the ground, traveling toward an unknown destination," Sir Gyzmo said, trotting happily alongside his beloved owner.

"It's not unknown at all. I know exactly where we are going," Willow advised.

As the moon slipped away and dawn broke over the mountains, Sir Gyzmo and Willow found themselves near the sleepy village of New Leaf, which had once held much promise for those who sought a new fresh way of life after Flowerville had been stricken with drought.

But promise and hope were not words that came to mind as the new view of the village emerged. The derecho had wreaked colossal destruction, and many of the huts were ruined.

"Do you think Wynter returned to New Leaf?" Sir Gyzmo inquired, looking sadly at the wreckage that had snuffed out any hope of the town's survival.

"I don't see her, but is that Aidan?" Willow gulped.

Crouching behind a cloudberry bush, Sir Gyzmo and Willow observed in silence as Aidan surveyed his damaged hut and his sheep bleated in the distance. He walked through the doorway of what remained of his home, then back out with his head dropped, looking as if the full weight of this devastating event rested upon his shoulders.

"Wynter isn't there," Willow whispered.

"I wonder where she is," Sir Gyzmo said. His voice trembling ever so slightly as he thought lovingly of the friend they had left behind in Snowdonia. He wondered if their paths might cross again. He certainly hoped so.

"Why do you think Aidan kept the truth of who he was from Wynter?" Sir Gyzmo questioned.

"If Wynter had known that Aidan was the same man who angered Dewdrop and caused the drought, she probably would not have chosen him for a mate. I think he was trying to influence Wynter into thinking he was someone that he wasn't by keeping secrets," Willow said sadly.

"It is indeed a tragedy," Sir Gyzmo responded.

"A tragedy that could have been avoided if the truth had been told," Willow answered.

As Willow rose from her hiding place behind the cloudberry bush, she felt no fear of the villain, Aidan. Reaching for her knapsack, she filled it full of the orange-colored cloudberries that tasted sweet, and tart like an apple and would sustain them with the energy needed for the remainder of their journey.

She turned toward Sir Gyzmo to make ready for their departure. He wore his holey stone necklace proudly on his chest. The fairy saddle she had braided for him from columbine and lavender flowers glistened in the sunlight, and his halter made from ferns and coyote willow rested in her tiny hands as she climbed upon his back.

"We go," Willow commanded with a strength that came from deep within. She had survived Aidan's relentless pursuit of her and her faithful companion, Sir Gyzmo, under the cloud-crazed skies of the Crooked Forest. She had survived the separation from Luna that Aidan had so heartlessly instigated and had cause her the greatest grief of her young life. She had proudly overcome many obstacles and realized her true potential and her destiny as a heroine.

Reunion

As Willow and Sir Gyzmo approached a grouping of hefty boulders, they appeared to be on a ceremonial path that was lined with a collection of remarkable ancient stones. Willow sensed the pulse of the earth's ley lines, and she instinctively knew that they had arrived at the portal to a parallel world where the earth's energy lines create a place of great power and protection to those attuned to the ancient ways and the natural world's forces.

Looking up, she spied a tree hole within a crooked pine. Two bare feet emerged from the tree hole, and Willows heart nearly stopped beating as her breath drew in, then abruptly ceased for several seconds as she studied the specifics of Luna's silhouette.

When she trusted herself to speak, she squeaked in a tiny voice, "Mother?

Luna peered down through the weighted branches that brushed the ground, forming an envelope of protection for the small creatures like herself, who called the Crooked Forest home.

"Willow?" her voice trembled as she slid from the tree hole, coming face to face with the daughter she loved so much.

Time stood still as the two embraced.

Luna looked younger and more beautiful than Willow remembered. Much time had passed since their separation, and even though her mother's image never left her memory, Willow was stunned by the exquisite features of her mother's face, which was far more beautiful in real life than the image Willow remembered.

The tears flowed along with happy laughter as the two struggled to find the words to express the elation they both felt for this reunion.

"I am so thankful that you found me!" Luna cried, wiping the tears that spilled from her eyes and poured down her cheeks.

"Once your location was revealed to me, Sir Gyzmo and I set out to find you," Willow sobbed.

Turning to Sir Gyzmo, Luna knelt beside the puppy that she had never met before today, as Sir Gyzmo lowered his head at Luna's soft touch as all gentlemanly, knightly dogs will do.

"My deepest gratitude to you, Sir Gyzmo, for protecting my precious daughter and counseling her during these grievous times. You will forever hold a cherished place in my heart," Luna whispered.

"It was the greatest reward of my life," Sir Gyzmo casually stated, as if saving young girls from harrowing times was nothing at all.

"You have fought for the greater good, and you have made a positive and caring difference in the world, Sir Gyzmo, and I will never be able to thank you enough," Luna wept.

"Being a part of this splendid reunion is all the thanks I need," the puppy spoke as only a true hero would.

As the trio sat upon the earth, a light evening breeze rustled the tall thin blades of Timothy grass, and the warm air dried their tear-stained faces. The air felt soft and pure. Bumblebees and butterfly wings murmured in the breeze as the rich nectar of the woodlands hung heavily around them. Happiness and joy filled the forest as Mother Earth celebrated this blessed reunion.

"It was difficult for me to find the strength to forgive Aidan for what he did to us," Willow confessed to her mother. "But I had to let it go, Mama. It made me someone that I did not want to be to stay angry at him for all eternity."

"An unforgiving spirit poisons one's own heart with bitterness," Luna answered.

"She has come so far since that first day that we met in the forest," Sir Gyzmo smiled.

"Heroes and heroines do not sacrifice themselves for others, and they never go against the greater good. Going against your destiny will only prevent you from living into your whole potential. And even though it is wise to never forget a betrayal, it does not mean that you cannot find forgiveness for those who have betrayed you." Luna smiled lovingly at her precious daughter and the enchanted fairy dog.

"I believe I heard those same words from a wise woman I met who pointed me in the right direction after I first met Sir Gyzmo. That same woman taught me to read the clouds and instructed me on my journey." Willow smiled.

Luna smiled knowingly. "I am so glad you were guided by her."

As the earth children sat under the protective branches of the crooked pines, the mountain bluebirds sang above them, and the ripe orange-colored cloudberries glistened in the green meadows surrounding them.

Sir Gyzmo happily raced around where Luna and Willow sat, panting as his holey stone necklace bounced against his chest, and he smiled the biggest corgi smile ever. His precious Willow had been released from her great sadness and had been reunited with her mother. She had also miraculously found forgiveness in her heart for Aidan.

Now he was part of a family that was glued by a bond so strong that no test, trial, or tribulation would ever breach their unit. He would wake up every morning knowing that he had a special place within this family. A family that he vowed to protect for the remainder of his days so that they would never be separated from each other again.

Until we meet again.

Printed in the United States
by Baker & Taylor Publisher Services